KURT GETS TRUCKLOADS

This edition first published in 2013 by Gecko Press
PO Box 9335, Marion Square, Wellington 6141, New Zealand
info@geckopress.com

Distributed in New Zealand by Random House NZ
Distributed in Australia by Scholastic Australia
Distributed in the United Kingdom by Bounce Sales & Marketing

Original title: Kurt blir grusom

Text by Erlend Loe; illustrations by Kim Hiorthøy

A catalogue record for this book is available from the National Library of New Zealand

Translated by Don Bartlett
Edited by Penelope Todd
Typeset by Book Design, New Zealand
Cover design by Luke Kelly, New Zealand

Printed in China by Everbest Printing Co Ltd, an accredited ISO 14001 & FSC certified printer

This translation has been published with the financial support of NORLA

ISBN paperback: 978-1-877579-30-1

For more curiously good books, visit www.geckopress.com

KURT GETS TRUCKLOADS

ERLEND LOE

Illustrated by Kim Hiorthøy
Translated by Don Bartlett

GECKO PRESS

This is Kurt. He's a truck driver.

He's driven trucks for years and years. Almost since he was a boy. He has a fine yellow truck that he's mighty proud of. Every Sunday without fail he washes it. Sometimes he washes it in the middle of the week, too, say on Wednesday or Thursday, but then Kurt's wife tells him he's going too far and that no one else in the world could be so crazy about a truck. Kurt's is the finest, yellowest truck in the whole town.

As well as his truck, Kurt has a moustache and a wife he loves a lot. She's an architect called Anna-Lisa. Kurt and Anna-Lisa have three children. Helena is the eldest. She's eleven and quite plump. At first she was very thin

but she ate so much fish she grew plump. Then there's Kurt Junior. He's nine and loves fizzy drinks so much they sometimes call him Fizzy Kurt.

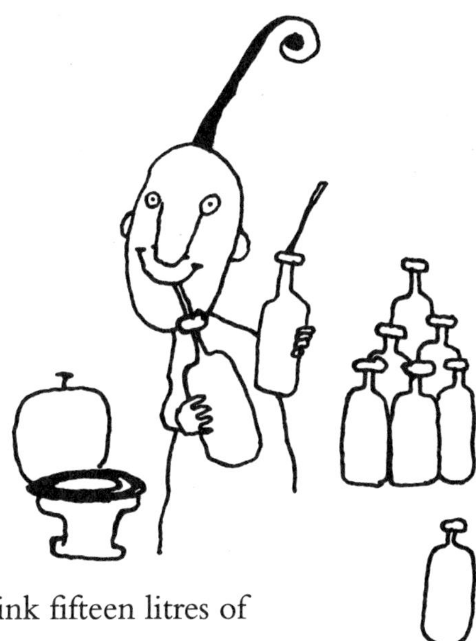

Fizzy Kurt can drink fifteen litres of fizz in an hour, no trouble. What's more, he has his own fizzy-drink maker. When he's not at school he's almost always in his room drinking fizz. He has to pee a lot, too. No one in the family pees as much as Kurt. Probably no one in the whole country does, but it's hard to say for sure because there might be other boys or girls who drink huge amounts of fizz without telling anyone.

The youngest member of the family is Bud. He's only a few years old and so small he hardly understands anything.

Some time ago the whole family went travelling. They drove all over the world in the truck, meeting lots of people and living off a huge fish that Kurt had been given by his boss. When the fish was all eaten up the family had to go home.

And now they've been home for quite a while. They're used to it. Kurt works at the harbour and Anna-Lisa designs houses, big and

small, for people to live in. The children go to school or kindergarten. They're a pretty normal family doing normal, everyday things.

In the evening the whole family sits in the living room watching something boring on TV. Bud is the first to get fed up. "This is so boring," he says. So Anna-Lisa puts him to bed and sees him off to sleep.

Then Kurt Junior is fed up. "What a stupid programme," he says. He takes his fizz with him and goes to bed.

Third to get fed up is Helena. "I can't be bothered watching this," she says. She takes a magazine and goes off to read in bed.

Almost at once Kurt and Anna-Lisa are fed up. "This is unbelievably boring," Kurt says.

"It certainly is," Anna-Lisa replies.

They switch off the TV, clean their teeth and go to bed.

Before they fall asleep Kurt and Anna-Lisa usually talk about how they'd like to travel again.

"Remember what it was like?" Kurt says.

"Of course I do," Anna-Lisa replies.

"I fancy doing a bit more."

"We can't afford it."

"That's true," says Kurt. "I wish we could though."

"Well, we can't," says Anna-Lisa.

Kurt thinks for a while. "Why is it some people have money and others don't?" he asks.

"Perhaps it's because some are lucky and others aren't," Anna-Lisa suggests.

"Which are we?" asks Kurt.

"Well, no one has to feel sorry for us," says Anna-Lisa. "We have all we need. Food, clothes, a truck and more. Lots of people are worse off than we are. We can't complain."

"I think we can complain a little."

"No," says Anna-Lisa. "I reckon we can't complain."

"But sometimes we're bored," Kurt says. "Surely that's not lucky?"

"You can't have fun all the time," says Anna-Lisa.

"I think you can," Kurt says. "If I had lots of money I'm sure I'd have fun all the time."

"Rubbish," Anna-Lisa says. "Anyway, I don't want all that much money. Just enough. So we can travel."

"I want lots of money," Kurt says.

Then he switches off the light and they go to sleep.

When they wake up the next morning they give each other a nice hug, then Kurt says there's something he's been wondering about.

"Go on," says Anna-Lisa.

"Why on earth wouldn't you want lots of money?" he asks. "Lots has to be better than a little."

"No, I don't think so," Anna-Lisa replies. "If you have too much money you can forget to be kind."

"Ha!" Kurt says. "I'll never forget to be kind. I've always been kind, and I'll never be anything but kind. You can count on that."

"Even if you get lots of money?" asks Anna-Lisa.

"Even if I get lots of money."

"Hmm," Anna-Lisa says, "but I heard of an ordinary man like you who got lots of money and turned nasty."

"How do you mean, nasty?" Kurt asks.

"Rotten," Anna-Lisa says. "He stopped being kind and was horrid to everyone."

"I'll never be like that."

"Promise?"

"It's an easy promise," Kurt says. "I won't ever have a lot of money."

"You never know," Anna-Lisa says.

Kurt makes himself a big packed lunch and clambers into the cab of his truck. Bud gets in, too, because Kurt has to take him to kindergarten. Bud's much too small to go on his own.

Bud sits on Kurt's lap and pretends he's driving. Bud likes sitting there. He's proud of his dad's truck. Kurt looks at his watch. He's always running late.

“How old are you actually?” Kurt asks.

“I must be two or three,” Bud answers.

“Is that so?” says Kurt. “We might start thinking about whether you’re almost ready to go to kindy on your own.”

“Might be,” Bud says.

They arrive at the kindergarten and Bud hops out. He stands and waves as Kurt heads for the harbour.

At the harbour Kurt says hello to the boss and all his workmates. Kurt’s boss is called Gunnar. He has a very high voice and is a really good guy.

"Morning, Kurt," Gunnar says. "Good to see you."

Right away Gunnar decides it's time to put the trucks to work. As usual, there are lots of boxes on the quay, and boats keep arriving with more. The quay is covered in boxes full of goods that people will buy.

But before they can buy them, Kurt and the other truck drivers move the boxes into a big warehouse out of the wind and rain. If it rains or the wind blows them around they can be spoilt, and then no one will want to buy them in the shops.

Kurt works all day. He moves hundreds of boxes, eats some crackers with cheese, then moves a few hundred more boxes. At last there are no boxes left. Work is over for the day.

Kurt parks his truck and goes for a little walk along the quay. He always does this when he's finished work. He spits into the water and stretches his arms. He looks along the quay. It seems to be empty. Kurt likes to see it empty. He walks on a bit. Walking is good for you.

Then Kurt notices something red and blue further along the quay. There's almost never anything way up there. But there is now, and whatever it is, it's red and blue. It can't be a box.

It's a man. A thin man in a blue uniform, lying on the quay. He has a big, red rucksack on his back and he seems to be asleep. Why would someone lie on the quay? Kurt's never seen anyone lying there before.

He walks over to the man, thinking that he'll have to wake him. You can't have a man lying on the quay. It's dangerous here. Besides, it's much better to lie under a roof. Suddenly the man gets up and heads for the edge of the quay. He's sleepwalking. That looks very dangerous. Kurt sets off at a run.

"Hey!" Kurt shouts. "Watch out!"

But the man doesn't hear. He walks straight off the edge of the quay and plunges into the water with a big splash.

Kurt thinks for two seconds, then jumps in. He swims straight down to the bottom.

The man's still asleep with the big rucksack on his back. He can't stay there. It's madness. If you sleep under water you'll end up drowning. Everyone knows that.

Kurt grabs the man round the middle and swims them up to the surface. The man's thin but he's very heavy, and Kurt only just makes it. Absolutely exhausted, he clutches at a ladder on the quayside and climbs up with the man and the rucksack, while gallons of water stream from them.

The sleeper has swallowed a lot of water. He coughs and splutters. Kurt lays him on the quay and slaps his face a couple of times until he comes round. Then he carries him to Gunnar's office.

Kurt and the thin man are soaked to the skin, cold and shocked. Gunnar rustles up some blankets and boiling hot coffee.

The thin man sheds a few tears thinking about what might have happened if Kurt hadn't been at hand.

"You saved my life," he says.

"Yes, I suppose I did," says Kurt.

"You saved my life," the man repeats.

"I heard what you said," says Kurt. "But why were you sleeping on the quay?"

The man tells them his name is George and that he works as a sailor on a ship that's just been to South Africa. Now he's on his way home for a few weeks' leave, but he was so tired he fell asleep the moment he got off the ship. He didn't even have time to call for a taxi. He's usually very tired when he comes home after long trips, he tells them, because he lies awake at night chatting and joking with the other sailors. But he's never been as tired as he was this time. It's the first time he's fallen asleep on the quay.

"You'll have to try to be a little less tired next time you come home," says Kurt.

"I suppose so," George agrees.

He drinks some coffee and dries his tears. He feels better now. He's not so upset. He's glad it turned out so well when it could have ended so badly.

Then George opens his rucksack and pulls out a big, wet, leather bag with a drawstring. He opens the bag and takes out a jagged, glassy stone about the size of a football.

"I want you to have this for saving my life," George says, giving the stone to Kurt.

"What am I supposed to do with it?" Kurt asks.

"You decide," says George. "In my family, when someone saves your life, you give him the finest thing you own. This stone is my finest possession. That's why I'm giving it to you. I found it high on a mountain in South Africa."

"What is it?" Kurt asks.

"It's a diamond."

"A diamond?"

George nods.

"Are you sure?" Kurt asks.

"Absolutely," George says.

"Thank you very much," says Kurt.

"I'm the one thanking *you*," George says. "And now I must go home and sleep." He gets up and thanks Gunnar for the coffee.

"My pleasure," Gunnar says.

Then George catches a taxi home. Kurt smiles and tosses the diamond in the air twice before putting it back into the leather bag.

"Well, you were lucky," Gunnar says.

Kurt nods. "But what can you do with a diamond?" he asks.

"I don't know," says Gunnar. "You could put it round your neck or in a drawer. There's actually a lot you can do with a diamond. You could even sell it and get some money for it."

"Did you say money?" says Kurt.

Kurt gets into his truck and drives to pick up Bud. He's pleased and proud. After all, it's not every day you're given a fine diamond.

On the way he pops in to a jeweller's. It's a little shop with a display counter and a man behind it. The display is half full of rings and gold and silver jewellery. The man looks bored. Kurt holds the bag with the diamond behind his back.

"Are you a jeweller?" he asks.

"Yep," says the man.

“Guess what I have here,” Kurt says.

The jeweller shrugs. “Probably a silver nugget,” he says.

“Nope,” Kurt says.

“Maybe some gold then?”

“Not exactly,” says Kurt.

“Well, I give up,” the jeweller says.

Kurt takes out the diamond and puts it on the counter where it gleams and glints.

The jeweller clutches his forehead and cries out. Then he faints. Kurt runs and fetches a glass of water to tip over the jeweller’s face. He fetches more and eventually the jeweller comes to. The jeweller gets up and walks around the diamond, clapping his hands. Then, breathing heavily, he peers at the diamond through a little tube. Afterwards he weighs the diamond and says, “Hmmm.” Then he examines it again. Finally he gives another shout.

“Fantastic!” he says.

“Well?” asks Kurt. “Is it a good diamond?”

"My good man," the jeweller says, "this diamond is not only good, it's the biggest and the best I've seen in the whole of my long life. It's an unbelievably good diamond, and I'd like to buy it."

"Really? You'd like to buy it?"

The jeweller starts writing numbers on a piece of paper. He adds and subtracts. It takes a long time.

"This diamond is worth fifty million dollars," he says at last.

"Fifty million?" repeats Kurt.

"Yep," the jeweller says.

Kurt thinks for a bit. "Do you consider that a lot of money?" he asks.

"I consider it a great deal of money," says the jeweller.

Kurt thinks for a bit longer. "If I have fifty million, am I rich?" he asks.

"If you have fifty million, you're the richest man in the whole city," the jeweller says.

"Good," says Kurt. "That's exactly what I want to be."

So Kurt sells the diamond to the jeweller. The jeweller opens a large safe and takes out a whole stack of money. He counts it and gives it to Kurt.

"Have you got a trailer?" Kurt asks.

The jeweller nods and runs into the backyard to fetch the trailer he uses when he buys gold and silver in foreign countries. He gives it to Kurt.

The trailer is filled to overflowing with money. The notes tower five metres into the air. Kurt has to tie them all down with several metres of rope. Then he attaches the trailer to his truck and climbs into the cab.

"It was a pleasure doing business with you," the jeweller says.

"And with you, too," says Kurt.

"By the way," the jeweller says, "have you ever had a lot of money before?"

"No," says Kurt.

"Then I suggest you take it slowly," the jeweller says. "It's not easy to manage a lot of money all at once."

"Thanks for the tip, but don't worry," says Kurt. "I'm as kind as the day is long. Always have been. I'm incredibly nice."

"Maybe so," the jeweller replies, "but strange things can happen to people who strike it rich. If I were you I'd be extra careful."

"I will be," Kurt says. And then he starts his truck and drives down the street with fifty million in the trailer.

On his way to the kindergarten Kurt is stopped by a police officer whose moustache is twice as thick as Kurt's.

The officer strolls around the truck and trailer twice, stroking his moustache.

"You're overloaded," he says.

"Think I've got too much, do you?" Kurt says with a laugh. "I don't think so." Then he looks at his watch. "Anyway, I don't have time to talk to stupid policemen," he says.

"It's forbidden to call policemen stupid," the officer says. "I'm afraid I'll have to fine you five hundred dollars."

"Ha! Is that all?" Kurt says. He calls the officer stupid again, and idiotic.

The officer takes out a calculator and does his sums. "That'll be fifteen hundred," he says.

Kurt takes out a pair of scissors and cuts off the ends of the officer's moustache.

"That was nasty," the officer says. "I'm afraid I'll have to fine you again. Is this your money, by the way?"

"Of course it is," Kurt says.

"You didn't steal it then?" the officer asks.

"No, I didn't steal it," says Kurt. "And you should watch yourself, because I'm rich and if you go on giving me cheek I might buy the whole police station and put you and all your friends in prison."

"Well, well," says the officer. He doesn't sound scared. "Anyway, you're driving with a high load, and that's against the law. I'll have to fine you for that, too."

Kurt looks at his watch again. He's very late. Bud will have been waiting for a long time already.

"I don't have time for this," he says. He takes a wad of thousand-dollar notes from the trailer and stuffs it into the officer's breast pocket. "Was there anything else? Kurt asks, patting the officer's cheek.

The officer nods. "You must put up a 'Heavy Load' sign before you drive any further," he says.

"Fine," says Kurt. He makes himself a sign, mounts it on the front of the truck, and quickly sets off for the kindergarten.

When Kurt arrives, Bud is sitting alone in the sandpit. He's plastered his face, mouth and inside his clothes with sand and mud. The other children were picked up hours ago.

"That's so like you," Kurt says. "Just because I'm a few hours late you make yourself all mucky like a stupid little baby. Won't you ever grow up?"

Bud shakes his head. "Why are you so late?" he asks.

Kurt brushes sand and mud off Bud's face and he tells him how he was stopped by a ridiculous policeman, but how he's now the richest man in the city. Then he lifts Bud up and dances round with him in the sand pit singing, "Money, Money, Money," a song Bud's never heard before.

"Are you Daddy's little boy?" Kurt asks. Bud nods. "Great," says Kurt, "because things are looking up."

While he drives, Kurt lets Bud sit on top of the money. Bud holds out his arms and pretends to fly all the way home.

When Kurt and Bud arrive, Kurt Junior's mouth is full of fizz as usual. Seeing the pile of money, he's so surprised he spurts fizz all over the desk, school books, carpet and furniture in his room.

Anna-Lisa storms in.

"Yuk!" she shouts. "You've done it again! How long do you plan to go on drinking this disgusting stuff?"

"For a while yet," Kurt Junior says. Then he points through the window, to the truck and trailer.

Anna-Lisa sees all the money and says "good heavens" and "well, I never" and becomes so flustered and her throat becomes so dry that she asks Kurt Junior for a swig of fizz, and she's never done that before.

Kurt Junior, Anna-Lisa and Helena charge out of the house. They stand watching as Kurt and Bud shovel the money into the garage.

"For heaven's sake," Anna-Lisa says. "Have you struck it rich, Kurt?"

He nods.

"There must be millions here," says Helena.

"Fifty million," Kurt says proudly.

"Bless my soul," says Anna-Lisa.

Kurt Junior runs up and dives into the pile of money.

"Hey, hey, hey," Kurt says. "Careful. If you're going to swim in the money, put down your drink first."

Kurt Junior puts it down.

"Can I dive in too?" asks Helena.

Kurt nods. "We can all swim in it," he says. "But only in bare feet."

So they all take off their shoes and socks and dive in. It's great fun. They throw notes about and swim through the money. Anna-Lisa goes wild. "Look at me!" she cries. "Look now!" She swims madly on her back, and jumps up and down in the pile of notes. But after she's swum and played for a while she can't help wondering.

"Hey, Kurt," she says.

"Yep," he says.

"I'm just wondering about this money. I mean, is your money my money?"

"Well, yes and no," Kurt replies.

"Mostly yes or mostly no?" Anna-Lisa asks.

"Mostly no," Kurt says. "You said you didn't want much money."

"But that was yesterday."

"It doesn't matter when it was," Kurt says. "You're a grown-up. You can't go changing your mind all the time. You said you didn't want much money, and I said I wanted as much as possible. So it makes sense that I have lots and you have a little. That's life," Kurt says. "It's tough."

"Did I really say I didn't want money?" Anna-Lisa asks.

"Yes," Kurt says. "But, hey, I don't want to be greedy."

He takes four hundred-dollar notes from the pile and gives one each to Anna-Lisa and the children.

"You can have fun with this or buy yourselves something nice," he says.

"Thank you very much," Kurt Junior and Helena say.

"Greedy guts," Anna-Lisa mumbles.

And Bud is speechless. He's never been given so much money. Besides, he has a mouthful of notes because, as you know, small children are always putting things in their mouths.

In bed that night, trying to sleep, Anna-Lisa is worried. She asks Kurt what he's going to do with all the money.

"I'm going to have fun," he says.

"All the time?" Anna-Lisa asks.

"Every hour and every second," Kurt says.

"How will you do that?"

"I'll buy expensive things," Kurt says.

"Is that fun?"

"I hope so," Kurt says.

"Hmm," says Anna-Lisa. "As long as you don't turn nasty."

“If you go on nagging, it won’t be at all surprising if I do,” Kurt says and he falls asleep.

Anna-Lisa bites her nails for quarter of an hour but then she falls asleep, too.

Next morning, Kurt doesn’t go to the harbour. Now that he has so much money it seems pointless to work. He sends Bud to kindergarten by taxi and lies in bed until almost midday. Then he gets up and phones the people who make telephone directories and asks them to write “multi-millionaire” after his name, so that anyone calling him knows they’re not talking to any ordinary person.

Then he drives his truck to a garage and asks the mechanic to paint it gold.

Once that's done, Kurt goes to town and buys himself cigars, a suit and a mobile phone. Then he takes a seat in an elegant restaurant. He drinks a glass of champagne and eats caviar, and phones Gunnar to tell him he won't be coming to work any more.

"What, never?" Gunnar asks.

"Never," says Kurt. "I've been given some money, so I don't need to work."

"Congratulations," Gunnar says.

"Do you wish it was you?"

"I'm not sure," Gunnar replies.

Then Kurt writes a list of things he'd like to buy. It's harder than he thought. With so much money he can have everything he wants, but it would be stupid to buy everything, so he limits himself to things he really, really wants. He can leave the things he'd only quite like for another day. He has plenty of time. He's going to be rich for many years. Maybe forever.

Kurt writes his list while smoking a cigar, and when he's finished he goes out and buys every item on it.

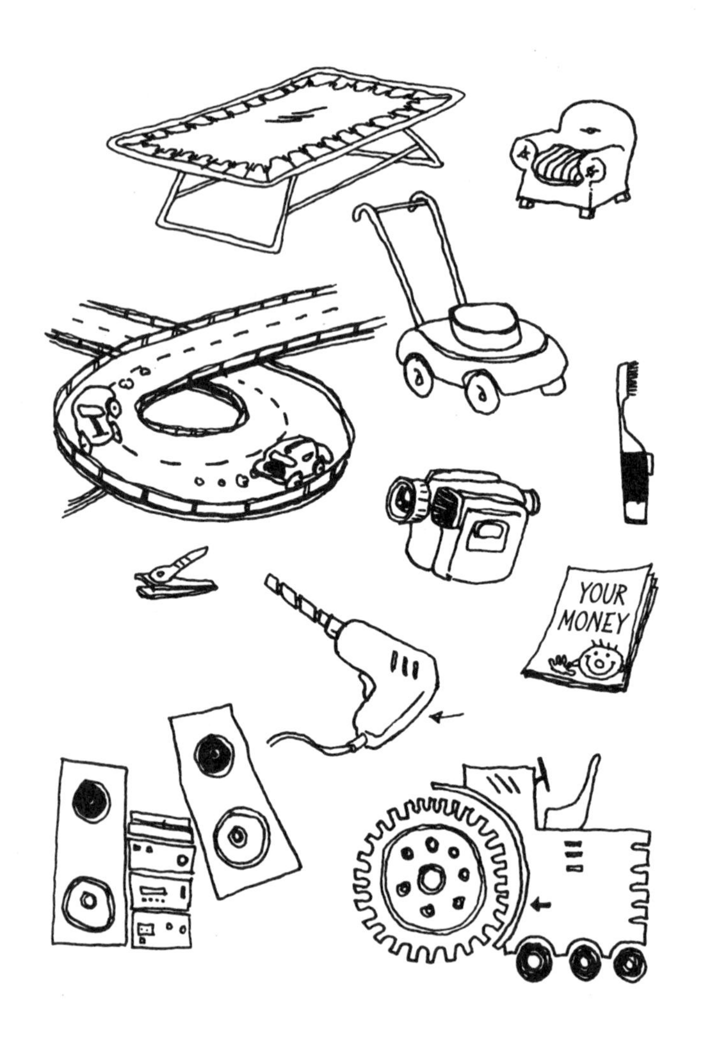
YOUR
MONEY

He buys a trampoline, a lawn mower, a big road-racing track, an electric toothbrush, a video camera, a drill, new furniture, a stereo set with large speakers, nail scissors, a magazine called *Your Money*, and a big machine that can saw through tarmac and concrete.

The goods are delivered to the door and Kurt claps his hands seeing them all together. Being rich is going to be great fun. Even more fun than he first thought. He takes off his suit jacket, loosens his tie and rolls up his sleeves. Then he gets to work.

First of all, he throws the old furniture out of the window and bores holes in it with the new drill. Then he sets it on fire. He's enjoying this.

Next, he carries in the new furniture and the stereo, and assembles the racing track. It's so big there's no space in the living room, so Kurt has to make a couple of holes in the walls to loop the track through Helena's bedroom and the kitchen. After that, Kurt mows the lawn and puts the trampoline beside the fish skeleton that's stood in the garden ever since the family came back from their trip a year ago. He parks the big machine outside the house, so it's ready for whenever he feels like sawing through tarmac or concrete. You never know when the urge will take you.

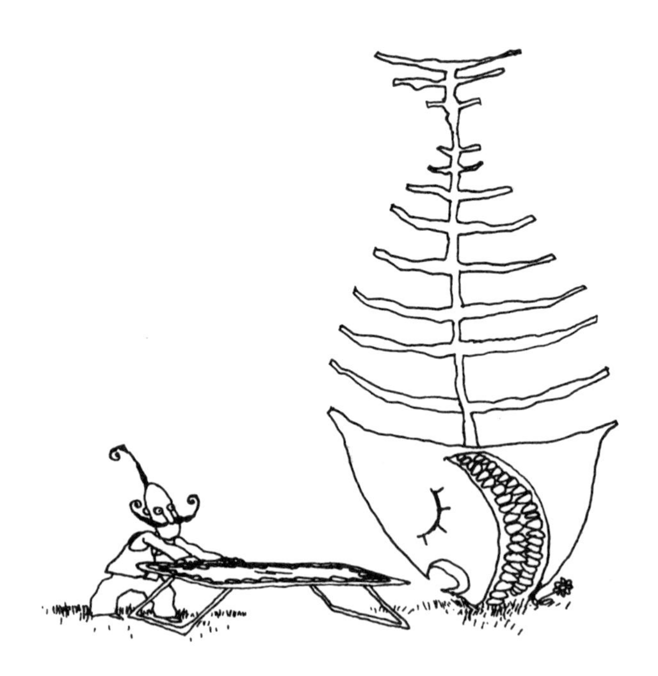

When Anna-Lisa, Bud, Kurt Junior and Helena come home, Kurt is on the new sofa grinning from ear to ear while smoking a cigar, cleaning his teeth with the electric toothbrush, playing with the race track and listening to loud music on the stereo. Before Anna-Lisa can say anything Kurt jumps up and films them with the video camera.

"Smile!" Kurt says. But only Bud smiles. Anna-Lisa and the others look annoyed. Anna-Lisa runs over to the stereo and turns the volume right down.

"Well, now I've seen everything," she says. "Just because you have money, do you think you can do whatever you like?"

"Pretty much," Kurt says.

Anna-Lisa shakes her head. "And what have you done with all the lovely old furniture?"

"I drilled holes in it and burnt it," Kurt says. "It was so old and boring. Don't get upset. I've bought new furniture."

"I think the new furniture's really ugly," says Helena.

"It's terrible," says Anna-Lisa. "And if I didn't know better I'd think you were turning nasty, Kurt."

"There's nothing nasty about this," Kurt replies. "I'm just having fun."

"Everyone who thinks Kurt's turning nasty put up your hand," Anna-Lisa says.

Kurt Junior and Helena put up their hands.

"See?" says Anna-Lisa.

"Hmm," says Kurt. Then he looks at Bud. "Do you think I'm nasty, Bud?"

Bud shakes his head.

"That's Daddy's boy," Kurt says.

But Anna-Lisa says Bud doesn't count because he's too small to know what's nasty and what isn't.

"You're just jealous," Kurt says. "And don't even ask if you can borrow my new things because from now on only Bud and I are going to have fun."

"Nasty," Anna-Lisa says.

"Mean," Kurt Junior says.

"Rotten," says Helena.

"And for your information, I'm going to give Bud ten thousand dollars a week for pocket money," Kurt says.

"Yay!" shouts Bud, but the others look even more annoyed.

Anna-Lisa shakes her head. "This is unbelievable," she says. She goes with Kurt Junior and Helena to the kitchen and slams the door behind her.

Bud sits on Kurt's lap. He's a bit upset because he doesn't like it when the family quarrels. Kurt comforts him and cleans his teeth with the electric toothbrush.

"Are you having a fight?" Bud asks.

"I'm definitely not fighting with anyone," Kurt says. "It's not my fault the others are in such bad moods, and are jealous."

"Whose fault is it?" Bud asks.

"Let's just forget about it for now," Kurt says. "Let's play with the race track and drill more holes in the wall. How about that?"

Of course Bud likes the sound of that. So they race cars and drill holes until late at night.

Meanwhile, Anna-Lisa, Kurt Junior and Helena grow crosser and crosser as they lie in bed listening to the racket in the living room. And on every circuit, the cars zoom through Helena's bedroom.

She can't get a wink of sleep. In the end, she's so wild she goes down to the cellar and yanks out the fuses. The whole house is plunged into darkness. The cars stop. The drill stops. The stereo stops working. But the electric toothbrush is battery-operated, so Kurt and Bud sit in

the darkness cleaning their teeth for a while before falling asleep on the sofa.

Next morning, Anna-Lisa feels cross the moment she opens her eyes. This has never happened before. She's often been cross during the day. That's quite usual. But to be cross first thing in the morning, that's not at all funny. She's cross about Kurt and his money, and she's also a bit cross with Bud, even though he's so small. She wakes Kurt Junior and Helena.

"Are you cross, too?" she asks them.

"Have a guess," they say.

It seems they're all cross.

"What shall we do about it?" Anna-Lisa asks when she's replaced the fuse and made breakfast.

"Don't know," Kurt Junior says.

"We'll have to wait until he's spent all the money," says Helena.

"Out of the question," says Anna-Lisa. "It'll take years to spend fifty million."

"Perhaps he was only being nasty yesterday?" Kurt Junior suggests.

"Let's hope so," says Anna-Lisa.

But just as she says it, drilling starts up in the living room. Kurt has woken up and is drilling holes in the new dining-room table.

"No, I think Kurt's going to be nasty today, too," Helena says.

"What a pain," says Anna-Lisa.

"Can't we do anything?" Kurt Junior asks.

"I really don't know," Anna-Lisa says, "but this can't go on, that's for sure. I'll try to figure out a plan today."

They clear away the breakfast things and go to work and school while Kurt sits on the sofa drilling holes until Bud wakes up.

Once Bud is wide awake and has done a bit of drilling, he asks if he can have his pocket money. Kurt gives him ten thousand dollars and Bud says thank you. Then he asks if he can take the drill to kindergarten because lots of children take their favourite toys. Kurt has a look on the box the drill came in, but it says nothing about children not being allowed to take it to kindergarten, so he says that's fine. Bud's happy and he promises he won't drill anything Kurt wouldn't drill.

"That's Daddy's boy," Kurt says, and he rings for a taxi to take Bud to kindergarten.

Once the taxi has gone Kurt puts on his tracksuit and goes out to jump on the trampoline. He's always wanted a trampoline, ever since he was a little boy. He loves jumping. After driving a truck, jumping is Kurt's favourite thing to do. He's done a bit on the lawn, but jumping from the ground you can't reach any great height so it becomes boring. With a trampoline you can jump really high: several metres, in fact.

Kurt jumps for hours. He jumps and jumps.

Sometimes he lands on his feet, sometimes on his bottom or stomach, but it doesn't hurt and each time he soars back into the air. When he's as high as he can go, he can see right over to the other side of town. It's great fun being rich. He can do as he likes all day, every day. Life couldn't be better.

After a while one of Kurt's neighbours strolls past.

“I hear you’ve struck it rich,” the neighbour says.

“Correct,” says Kurt. He keeps on jumping.

“Perhaps you could lend me some money then?” the neighbour asks.

“No,” Kurt says. “It’s my money and I don’t lend it. But if you go down to the quay and save someone from drowning you might earn yourself a diamond. Then you’ll be rich, like me.”

"Thanks for the tip," the neighbour says. "But how about the trampoline? You don't mind if I have a go, do you?"

"I'm afraid I do," Kurt says.

"Why?"

"Because I've decided only Bud and I are going to have fun with my things," Kurt says.

"I didn't realise you were so stingy," the neighbour says.

"I didn't realise you were so pushy," says Kurt.

The neighbour gets angry and takes the bus down to the quay to save someone from drowning so he can be rich, too, and jump on a trampoline all day.

Kurt goes on jumping for a while, but then he gets fed up. He sits on the lawn and reads his magazine called *Your Money*. There are tips in it to help rich people. It says that if you have lots of money but want even more, you can buy things cheaply and sell them at a high price.

That sounds like a fantastic idea, but Kurt's not sure he needs more money right now. He can do that in a few years when his pile has shrunk a bit. But he notices something in the magazine. All the people interviewed are directors and bosses who make all sorts of decisions, even though they don't have as much money as Kurt.

That doesn't seem fair. Kurt wants to make decisions as well. What's the point of having so much money if you spend your time drilling holes and bouncing on a silly trampoline? Kurt wants to decide things. He wants influence.

He lies back on the grass and looks up at the drifting clouds, thinking what fun it would be to make decisions. He'd like to make as many as possible. And quite important ones because if he's only allowed to decide on insignificant matters, that will be boring in the long term.

But who makes important decisions? Kurt's not sure. The king perhaps? But there's a king already, and besides, you have to be a prince before you can be a king, and Kurt is not and has never been a prince. So he'll have to think of something else.

Now, here's an idea: he can become Prime Minister. That must be the best. The Prime Minister makes an incredible number of decisions, and what's more is on TV almost every day. Kurt really likes the thought of that. He takes out his mobile phone and calls the Prime Minister. She sounds quite nice on the phone. "Hi," Kurt says, "my name's Kurt and I'd very much like to be Prime Minister."

"I see," says the Prime Minister.

"Do you make a lot of decisions?" Kurt asks.

"I decide absolutely everything," the Prime Minister says.

"Is that fun?" Kurt asks.

"It's great fun," she says.

“Do you earn a lot?” Kurt asks.

“I certainly do.”

“Do you buy things cheaply and sell them for more?” Kurt asks.

“No, I’ve never done that,” says the Prime Minister, “but I’ll give it some thought. It sounds like good advice.”

"But how do you actually become a Prime Minister?" Kurt asks.

"You have to talk a bit on TV and in the newspapers so that people begin to like you, and then you have to ask them to vote for you next time there's an election," she says.

"Is it long until the next election?" Kurt asks.

"No," says the Prime Minister. "It's not very long, but I can tell you right now that you don't have a chance because I'm very nice and extremely popular."

"So am I," says Kurt.

"Good luck then," the Prime Minister says.

"The same to you," says Kurt, laughing quietly as he closes his mobile and puts it in his pocket. This should be easy. He can hardly wait to start making decisions. He might become the richest and most influential man in the country, perhaps even the world.

While Kurt is lying on the grass and dreaming of becoming Prime Minister, Bud comes home from kindergarten. It's very early. He shouldn't be back for several hours, but here he is. Bud pays the taxi driver and gets out of the car. He looks upset.

In one hand is the drill and in the other a letter. He walks slowly towards Kurt.

"Hi there," Kurt says. "You're a bit early, aren't you?"

"I've been sent home," Bud says.

"You've been sent home?" Kurt echoes.

"Yes," says Bud, and he starts crying.

"Did you do something naughty?" Kurt asks.

"Yes."

"What did you do?" Kurt asks.

Bud doesn't answer.

"Don't you want to tell me?" Kurt asks.

"Not really," says Bud, with tears flowing down his cheeks.

Kurt comforts him and says it can't be that bad. "You can tell me," Kurt says. "I promise not to get angry."

So Bud gives him the letter. It's from the head of the kindergarten and it says that Bud drilled holes in the kindergarten and in the teachers' running shoes, and that furthermore he was unkind to the other children and that he can't come back until he's sure he is going to be kind again.

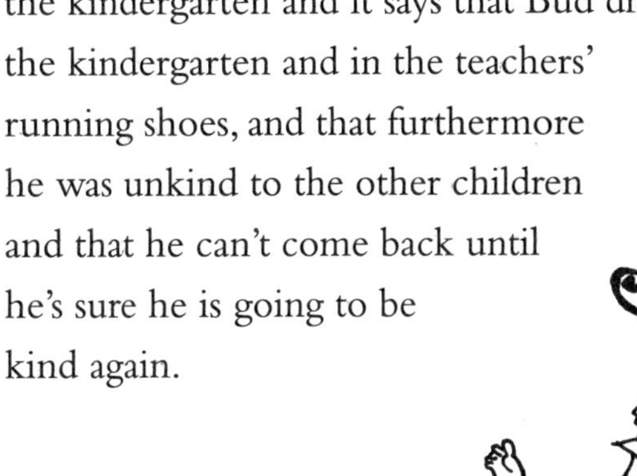

"Hmm," Kurt says. "This is not good. Were you very unkind to the other children?"

"Not *very*," Bud says.

"What did you do?"

"I bought some sweets," Bud says. "And then I didn't share them."

"How many did you buy?" Kurt asks.

"A thousand dollars' worth."

"Hmm," Kurt says. "And then you drilled holes in the teachers' running shoes. Didn't you promise me not to do anything I wouldn't? Do you really think I'd drill holes in the teachers' shoes?"

"I wasn't sure," Bud says.

"Well," Kurt says, "I suppose it's not easy to know where to drill when you're so small."

"No," Bud says.

"Are you nice again now?" Kurt asks.

"I'm not sure," Bud says. "Can I stay home with you until we're sure?"

"Of course you can," says Kurt. "Because you're Daddy's boy, aren't you?"

"Yes," says Bud. Then he looks around. "What shall we do?"

Kurt tells him he's going to be Prime Minister and appear on TV and make all sorts of decisions. Bud thinks that sounds like a great idea.

"Do you know anything about politics?" Kurt asks.

"No."

"I suppose you can't help that, considering how small you are," Kurt says, irritated. "But maybe you can help me anyway."

"Maybe," agrees Bud.

"You can be my campaign manager," Kurt says. "It should be pretty simple. You just have to phone all the

TV and radio stations and tell them your dad would make a good Prime Minister. Want to do that?"

"I think so," Bud says. "But do you think you would be a good Prime Minister?"

"Of course," says Kurt.

They drive to town and buy Bud a little suit with a tie, and patent leather shoes. They also buy a little mobile phone. Bud looks very stylish. He looks like a hunk, and when he stands talking on the phone grown-up women whistle at him. Bud whistles back because he's so small he doesn't know what it means when people whistle like that.

Then they get to work. First, they make a poster to stick on walls all over the country. It costs a lot of money to make this kind of poster and even more to stick it on all the walls, but Kurt has money.

They take a picture of Kurt sitting in his truck pointing at the camera and grinning with freshly cleaned teeth. The poster needs words as well. It's not easy to decide what they should be. Kurt wants to write:

Kurt's the best
The very best
Kurt-Kurt-Kurt
Best-Best-Best
Hip-Hoo-Ray

But Bud doesn't think this is a good idea.

Kurt has a think and phones some experts, and in the end they write:

One World, One Future
Vote for Security, Vote for Kurt

When Anna-Lisa and the others come home they're surprised to find that Kurt and Bud have stopped drilling and making a racket.

"Have you finished drilling?" Anna-Lisa asks.

"Ha!" Kurt snorts. "That's what I *used* to do. Now I'm going to be the next Prime Minister and appear on TV and make decisions, so I have better things to do than jumping and drilling."

"Are you going to be Prime Minister?" Anna-Lisa asks.

"Yep," says Kurt, "and you're going to vote for me."

"We'll see about that," Anna-Lisa says. "But I'd much rather have you trying to become Prime Minister than hanging around being nasty. Perhaps I won't have to kick you out after all."

"Were you thinking of kicking me out?" Kurt asks.

"I was, actually," says Anna-Lisa.

"Well, I've never heard such nonsense," Kurt says. "No one throws a Prime Ministerial candidate out of their house."

"There aren't many Prime Ministerial candidates who drill and make a racket," Anna-Lisa says.

"I told you I've stopped all that," says Kurt.

"I hope so."

And then Kurt Junior makes fizz for everyone and they sit in the living room.

They're a family again, and Kurt promises he'll buy more new furniture and he won't drill into it.

Now comes a busy time for Kurt and Bud. The poster with the photo of Kurt appears all over the country, and people start noticing it. Every day for several weeks

Bud gets on the phone and talks to the newspapers, TV and radio. He tells them about Kurt: how good he is at driving his truck and how kind he is. Now and then there's a question he can't answer, so he tells them to wait while he talks to Kurt, the Prime Ministerial candidate.

"Hey, Kurt," Bud says. "I've got someone here asking what you think about agriculture and fisheries."

"I think both are very important," Kurt says. "No, wait a moment. Say I think both are vital in a society like ours, and then say I love fish, and furthermore I'm prepared to spend my own money if farmers and fishermen feel they're short of anything."

Bud repeats what Kurt has said and it goes into the papers and onto the radio.

"Would you really spend your money if farmers or fishermen were short of something?" Bud asks afterwards.

"No way," says Kurt. "It was just something to say. After all, I say a lot. You have to if you want to become Prime Minister."

"I thought so," Bud says. "But what if someone remembers what you said?"

"I'll deny it," says Kurt.

As the elections get closer, Kurt and Bud buy sunglasses and hire a jet for travelling around the country to meet as many people as possible. Bud has had pamphlets, badges and baseball caps made to give away on streets and at markets while talking to people about what a good Prime Minister Kurt would make.

And Kurt makes speeches saying how concerned he is about unemployment and good roads and people enjoying themselves. He tells them that everything will be better and that we all have to take care of the family and the environment.

"You didn't say anything about the elderly," an old lady says.

"Didn't I?" Kurt says. "Well, I'm glad you mentioned it because caring for old people is probably my number-one concern." Then he kicks Bud in the shin because Bud's so small he's forgotten to mention the elderly in the pamphlet.

Many people are worried, and they come up to Kurt to ask if he can help them with a variety of matters when he becomes Prime Minister. One doesn't have enough money; another wants someone to build a tunnel so he doesn't have to drive so far to work; a third thinks there are too many dogs on the loose in the forest.

Kurt tells everyone not to worry and that everything will be all right.

"I'll sort it out," he says. "Of course! Vote for me and it'll be all right. And don't forget that a vote for Kurt is a vote for a secure future!"

And all the time Bud is there in the background, distributing leaflets or talking to important people on his mobile phone. But he's stopped whistling at women, because Kurt told him what it means and Bud wouldn't dream of being interested in women. Anna-Lisa and Helena are the only girls he likes. He thinks all the others are stupid, but of course that's because he's so small and childish.

The day before the election, all the Prime Ministerial candidates have to discuss things on TV so that the viewers can decide who they'll vote for. Kurt has to put on make-up and sit in a chair and drink water with several spotlights shining on his face. The woman he spoke to on the phone, the present Prime Minister, wants to run a second time and she talks non-stop. Kurt can hardly get a word in, and when he's asked a question he finds it hard to answer.

KURT
KURT
TV
TV

"Well, well, Kurt. What do you think about whaling?" asks the TV host.

"Whaling?" Kurt says, taking a large swig of water. "Whales are big animals of course, and they taste good, too, but they're happiest when people aren't harpooning them. It's a difficult issue. Now and then, perhaps, we can kill the odd whale, but as a rule I think we should leave them alone."

"Thank you, Kurt," says the host.

Then all the other candidates give their opinions on whaling. Kurt is bored. But there are more questions to answer.

"What would you do about unemployment, Kurt?" the host asks.

"I think people who have no work or money should buy goods cheaply and sell them at a profit," Kurt says. "I've read about it in a magazine, and I believe it's good advice."

"I see," says the host, while some of the other

candidates laugh and nudge each other. "But what about children and young people?"

"Yes, what about them?" Kurt says.

"What will you do for them, Kurt?"

"Children and young people?" Kurt takes another swig of water. He swigs again, and looks nervously into the camera. "To tell you the truth, I haven't thought about them," he says. "But I've thought about plenty of other things. And I'm very concerned about the future."

"I'm sure you are," says the host.

And then the programme is over and the candidates go home to bed excited about the election the following day. Kurt isn't very pleased with his performance, but he's confident that the posters he's put up all over the country will do the job.

When they go to bed that night Kurt asks if Anna-Lisa thinks he'll be the next Prime Minister.

"I don't think so," she says. "What do you think?"

"I think I will be," Kurt says.

"Will you be very disappointed if you're not?" asks Anna-Lisa.

"Yes."

"Will you be angry?" she asks.

"Yes."

"But you won't be nasty, will you?" Anna-Lisa asks.

"I'm going to sleep now," says Kurt.

The next day, Kurt and Anna-Lisa vote. The children stay at home because they're too young to vote, especially Bud who is, as we know, the youngest member of the family.

Kurt votes for himself. It's a wonderful feeling to take the slip with his name on and place it in the envelope and put it in the metal box in the middle of the room. On their way home, Anna-Lisa refuses to tell him who she voted for.

"Come on, you can tell me," Kurt says.

"I will not," says Anna-Lisa.

"Was it me?" Kurt asks. "You can tell me if it was me."

"I'm not saying."

"I think you voted for me," says Kurt.

But Anna-Lisa didn't vote for Kurt. And nor did anyone else, because when the votes are counted it turns out that Kurt only received one vote and that was his own. And the candidate who became Prime Minister was already the Prime Minister.

When Kurt hears this, at first he's very disappointed and then he's angry. Then he goes berserk. He runs around the house yelling and drilling holes in the fridge, even though he promised he'd stop using the drill.

"I'll show them!" he shouts. "I'll show them! I've never been so badly treated in my life. I would have been a great Prime Minister, I would have been the best. I'll blimmin' well show them."

Kurt runs outside and gets into the big machine that saws up tarmac and concrete. He switches on the radio and finds a channel with loud music, then he starts the engine and begins to cut his way down the street. He saws the street and the whole neighbourhood in half. Going flat-out, he chops cars in half, and garages and football pitches.

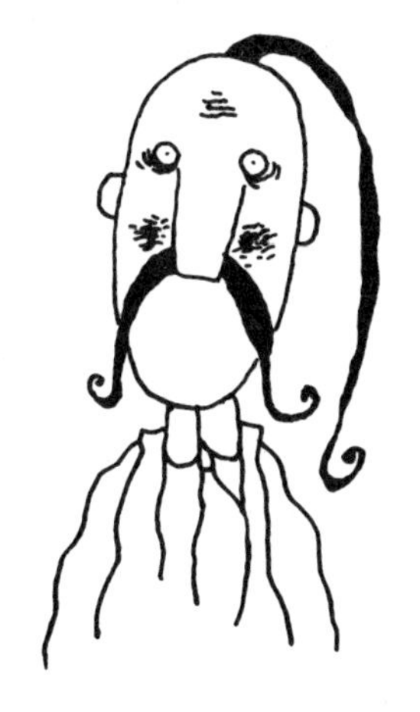

People are scared out of their wits. They hide in their cellars, and some ring the police to tell them there's a nasty, crazy man on the loose.

Kurt puts the machine into fourth gear and cuts up the motorway. He destroys everything in his path. He saws up bridges and traffic lights and petrol stations as he shouts, "I'll show the lot of you!"

Kurt sees helicopters hovering above him. He hears sirens coming from every side, but they only make him drive faster. Suddenly there's a barricade up ahead. A big police bus blocks the whole road, and lots of policemen stand by, ready to arrest him.

But Kurt doesn't stop. He saws right through the bus, scattering police officers in all directions. He leaves the motorway and heads for the city centre.

At home Bud, Kurt Junior and Helena are watching it all on TV.

“No, no, no!” says Anna-Lisa. “This is dreadful. Maybe I should have voted for him after all.”

“Daddy’s gone bananas,” Helena says.

“I think he’s doing the right thing,” says Bud.

As they sit there, the telephone rings. Anna-Lisa answers. It's the radio. They want her to say something to make Kurt stop. Anna-Lisa agrees to help.

"Kurt," she says, "this is Anna-Lisa. If you hear this, please think about what you're doing. Sooner or later you'll have to stop. You might as well stop now. The whole family's watching you wreck things. There's an awful lot of wreckage. Not everyone can be Prime Minister, Kurt. But you're certainly the best truck-driver in the world, and I want you to know I love you even though you're nasty and slightly crazy. Stop the machine and come home. We miss you."

The radio people thank Anna-Lisa and she sits back in front of the TV wondering whether Kurt has heard her.

But Kurt hasn't heard. His machine is making so much noise he can hardly hear the radio at all. And he's still just as furious. He saws his way down to the city.

Hot dog wagons and newspaper kiosks are sawn in two, but no one gets hurt because everyone's been told to stay indoors.

The police have put up more barricades, but Kurt cuts through them, too. Nothing can stop him.

STOP

Kurt is infuriating a lot of people. He's destroyed houses and roads and expensive cars. Almost everyone in the country is sitting in front of a television, following events and waiting for the police to arrest him.

Kurt reaches the city centre. He chops through the palace gardens, flinging birds and trees about. It's a sorry sight.

The king himself comes out onto the balcony and silently shakes his head. This is the worst thing he's ever seen, and he's seen a lot.

Kurt takes his time sawing up the square in front of the palace before heading down Karl Johan Street, aiming for the train station and the parliament buildings. Now he reckons he can really do some damage. The woman elected to be Prime Minister stands with friends

drinking champagne and celebrating her victory as Kurt approaches. He's going full tilt and thunders into the wall with a great crash. He starts sawing. The wall is thick and it takes time. Suddenly, over a hundred police cars hurtle round the corner and Kurt is surrounded. But he won't stop sawing. Soon he'll be through the wall, then he'll chop the great hall into smithereens along with all the stupid old paintings hanging there.

But with only centimetres to go, the big road-cutting machine runs out of petrol. The huge saw stops rotating and Kurt sits for a few seconds looking silly before the police make a charge, grab him and put him in handcuffs.

"Got you now!" says the Chief of Police.

"How incredibly annoying," Kurt says. "I was only millimetres away."

The Prime Minister and her friends come out and survey the damage.

"Goodness," says the Prime Minister. "Was it really

you doing this? You're the worst loser I've ever met."

Kurt says nothing.

"You're neither kind *nor* popular," she says. "You should be ashamed of yourself!"

Kurt has to spend the night in prison. It's the saddest place he's ever spent a night, and after only fifteen minutes he regrets what he's done.

Next day, there's a picture of Kurt on the front page of the paper. LOST ELECTION AND TURNED NASTY, it says.

People who went to school with Kurt are interviewed and say they can't understand how he could do something so nasty; as a child he was always so kind and happy. It's no fun at all for Kurt, reading that.

And then there has to be a trial because no one's allowed to cut up streets and towns just because they didn't become Prime Minister.

"Well, Kurt. Have you been this nasty before?" the judge asks.

"No, never," says Kurt, "and I'm really sorry."

"Are you quite sure?"

"Yes," Kurt says. "I'll never do it again. I wasn't myself."

"You weren't yourself?" the judge says. "Then who were you?"

"I don't know. I was so furious I couldn't even think," Kurt says. "Haven't you ever felt like that?"

"In fact, I have," the judge says.

"Well, there you go."

"I'm going to give you a choice, Kurt," says the judge. "Either you pay forty million dollars in compensation, or you go to prison."

"I'll pay," Kurt says. "I don't want to go to prison. It's the saddest, most boring place I've ever been."

"And another thing," says the judge. "You'll never be allowed to drive a road-cutting machine again."

"What about a truck?" Kurt asks, anxiously. "Am I allowed to drive a truck?"

"You can drive a truck as much as you like," the judge says.

"Thank you very much," says Kurt.

He catches the bus home, collects forty million dollars, goes to the post office and pays the fine.

Now there's only a little money left. Kurt gives it to Anna-Lisa and says she can decide what to do with it because he's had enough of money for now.

"I'll put it in the bank and spend it on something nice for all of us," Anna-Lisa says.

"Do that," Kurt says.

And then everyone in the family hugs and is happy again.

"Now we're back where we started," says Anna-Lisa. "We're friends and we don't have much money and not one of us is nasty. Imagine you turning nasty, Kurt!" she says.

"Yes, it's strange," Kurt says. "Who would have thought I had it in me?"

They all sit down and watch something boring on TV while eating chips and drinking the fizz that Kurt Junior made in his fizzy drink maker. And gradually, as they get tired, they go to bed. First Bud, then Kurt Junior, then Helena, and last of all Kurt and Anna-Lisa.

When they're lying in bed, Kurt asks Anna-Lisa if she'd like to hear something strange.

He says, "When I was in the road-cutting machine it was as though I could hear your voice. Isn't that odd?"

"In fact, it's not so odd," Anna-Lisa says, "because I spoke to you on the radio. If you'd listened harder you might have stopped sooner."

"Have you ever sawn through tarmac and concrete?" Kurt asks.

"No."

"I thought not," Kurt says. "Because if you had, you'd know you can hardly hear a thing and you would've spoken louder. We'd have a bit more money left if you'd spoken louder. So it's actually slightly your fault I kept going."

"You know what?" says Anna-Lisa. "That's the cheekiest thing I've ever heard! *You* were the one who sawed up the road, and if you say it's my fault I'll get mad and stay mad for years."

Kurt won't risk that, so he admits it was his fault and they both go to asleep.

Next morning, Anna-Lisa asks Kurt what he's going to do now.

"I'll probably wander down to the harbour and see if there's any work for me," Kurt says. "And Bud will have to go back to kindergarten. I'm tired of seeing him in a suit and sunglasses."

Then Kurt takes the truck and drives Bud to kindergarten just as he used to before he became rich.

Kurt gives the kindergarten teachers new running shoes and apologises for Bud's bad behaviour.

"Is he nice again now?" the teachers ask.

"Very nice," Kurt says.

"What about you? Are you nice again?" the teachers ask.

"I'm nice again, too."

"That's good," the teachers say.

Then Bud runs off to play with the other children. It's great to be back at kindergarten.

Kurt drives down to the harbour and goes into Gunnar's office.

"Are you coming back now?" Gunnar asks in his high voice.

"Yes, I'm coming back now," Kurt says.

"Welcome, then," says Gunnar. "I hear you've been pretty nasty."

"Yes," says Kurt. "I tried to become Prime Minister."

"That didn't go so well though," Gunnar says.

"No, I only got one vote, and then I got into trouble for being nasty."

"It can happen to the best of us," Gunnar says.

"Apparently."

"And now you want to work?" Gunnar asks.

"I'd like to work, yes," says Kurt.

"Well then," Gunnar says, "there's plenty to do." He glances at his watch and says they might as well get started.

But before Kurt can stand, Gunnar looks up and coughs. "What did you do with that diamond, by the way?"

"You mean the big one?" Kurt asks.

"Yes, that one."

"I sold it and got lots of money for it," says Kurt.

"You sold it?" Gunnar says.

"Yes, and I became rich and wanted to be Prime Minister, and then I turned nasty," says Kurt.

"Ah, so that's how it all fits together," Gunnar says.

Kurt nods and strokes his moustache.

"It's amazing how rich and nasty you can become if you have a big enough diamond," he says.